Other Books by Patricia Reilly Giff:

The Gift of the Pirate Queen
Illustrated by Jenny Rutherford

Casey, Tracy, and Company
Illustrated by Leslie Morrill
Poopsie Pomerantz, Pick Up Your Feet
Love, From the Fifth-Grade Celebrity
Fourth-Grade Celebrity
The Girl Who Knew It All
Left-Handed Shortstop
The Winter Worm Business
Rat Teeth

The Abby Jones, Junior Detective, Mysteries
Illustrated by Anthony Kramer
Have You Seen Hyacinth Macaw?
Loretta P. Sweeny, Where Are You?
Tootsie Tanner, Why Don't You Talk?

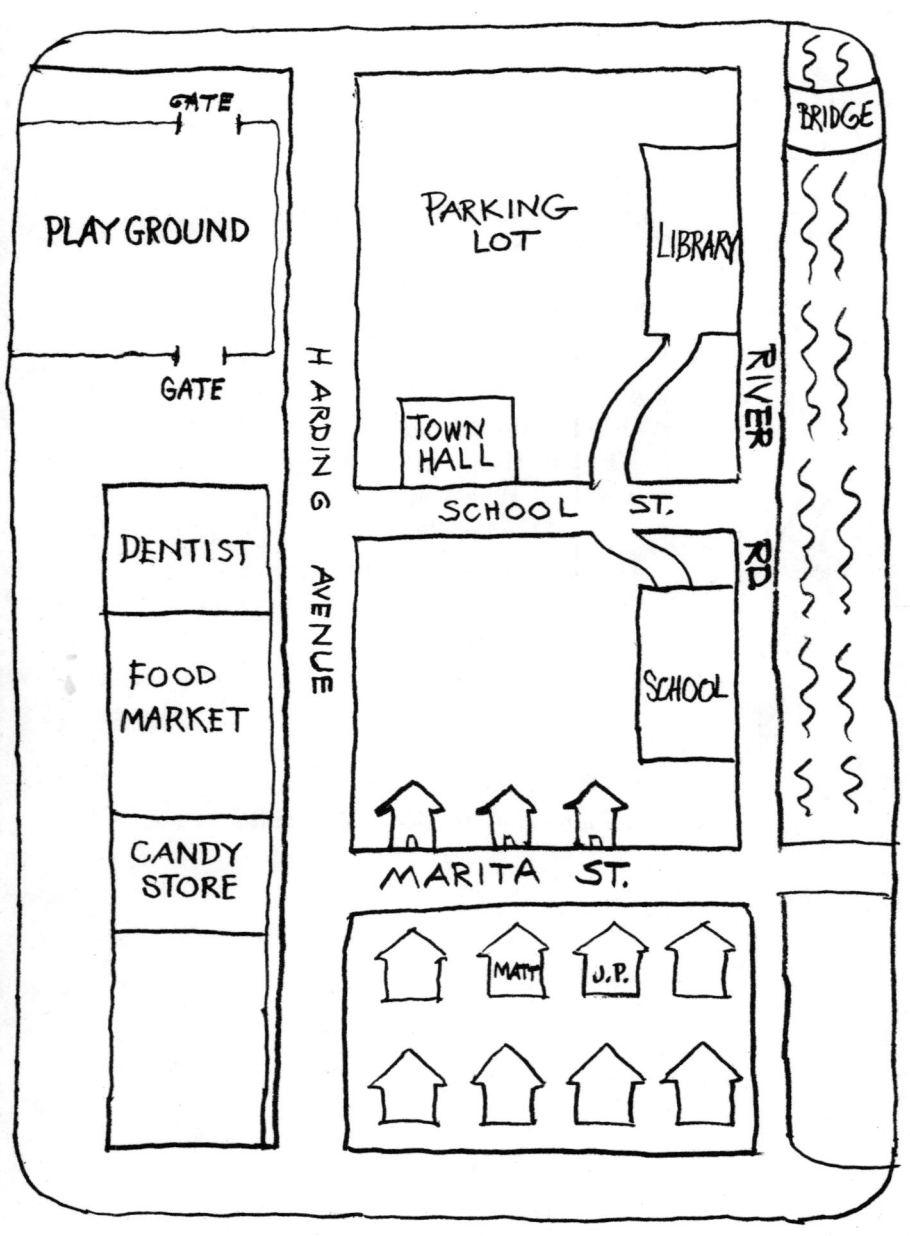

Matthew Jackson Meets the Wall

by Patricia Reilly Giff

Illustrated by Blanche Sims

Delacorte Press

For Bunny Gabel,
with love and gratitude

Published by
Delacorte Press
Bantam Doubleday Dell Publishing Group, Inc.
666 Fifth Avenue
New York, New York 10103

Library of Congress Cataloging in Publication Data

Giff, Patricia Reilly

   Matthew Jackson meets the wall / by Patricia Reilly Giff; illustrated by Blanche Sims.
     p.   cm.
   Summary: Matthew's family's moving from New York to Ohio is difficult enough as they leave behind good friends and memories, but the disappearance of their cat and a neighbor boy so tough he's called the "Wall" add to Matthew's anxieties.
   ISBN 0–385–29972–9
   [1. Moving, Household—Fiction.]   I. Sims, Blanche, ill.
II. Title.
PZ7.G3626Mat   1990
[Fic]—dc20   89–23699
                                            CIP
                                            AC

Manufactured in the United States of America

May 1990

10 9 8 7 6 5 4 3 2 1

BVG

1

"**I**'m starving to death," Matthew Jackson said from the back seat of his father's station wagon. He was holding a square white box on his lap. It said PIZZA CORNER, DEPOSIT, OHIO.

He wished he could tear the box open right this minute. He couldn't wait to sink his teeth into the hot tomatoes and stringy cheese. He leaned over to take a sniff.

On the floor of the car he could see Barney, his cat, twitching her tail. She must be starving too.

His older sister Cindy grinned at him. "You think anyone wants to eat that stuff after you've inhaled the whole thing?" Her freckled face was so close he could smell the tutti-frutti gum she had been chewing all day.

"The box is closed," Matthew said.

"Boxes closed, boxes closed," two-year-old Laurie sang from her car seat.

"Hold on another minute," their father said. "Not much more." They turned the corner. "Look, kids," he said. "There's the River Road School."

"Yuck-o," said Matthew. It was almost dark, but there were lights on in the schoolyard.

River Road School didn't look one bit like the Polk Street School. It was long and low, not tall with columns in front.

"Terrible," said Cindy. "I'm glad we don't start for another month."

Their father laughed. "I wasn't crazy about school either. Look, we just have to turn the corner, and we're there."

Matthew peered out the window into the darkness. He could see trees as his father swung into the turn, then a row of houses. The first one was white, the next was gray . . .

2

"Third one's ours," said his father. "The green one." He laughed. "Not so new. I guess it's a hundred years old."

Matthew rolled down the window. He stuck his head out for a good look. The house was tall and pointy with lots of skinny windows. It looked as if it were haunted.

"Beautiful," said his mother, "just beautiful."

"Yup," said Mr. Jackson. He pulled slowly into the driveway.

Matthew looked back at the street. It was too late for kids to be out. They were probably inside their tall pointy houses watching television. That's what his old friend Beast would be doing right now in New York. He'd be watching cartoons or a mystery, lying on his living-room floor. Maybe Emily would be there, too, or Timothy Barbiero. Lucky.

Matthew sighed. They'd driven about a million miles today, all the way from New York to Ohio, with only a couple of stops. One stop for peanut butter sandwiches and orange juice at the side of the road. Another stop a few minutes ago to get the pizza. A few stops in between to race into the bath-rooms on the highways while his father kept the car running.

That reminded him. "I'm first in the bathroom." He looked at Cindy.

"I knew it," she said. "You've been in about a hundred bathrooms today."

"Only fifty," said his father. He turned off the motor.

It felt strange without the car running. The hum and the feeling of moving were gone. Everything was still.

Then his father began to sing. "Be it ev-er so hum-ble, there's no-oh place like home."

"Sum-ble," Laurie sang.

Matthew swallowed. He wondered if this new house would ever seem like home.

His mother turned around. "Am I glad this ride is over!" She opened the banana clip that held her hair back, and shook her head. "Let's get out and take a look."

Matthew shoved the pizza box onto Cindy's lap.

"Grab this, will you? I'll carry Barney. I don't want her to get lost."

He picked up the cat, burying his face in her soft gray fur. Usually when he did that, she'd begin to purr. Not tonight though. She'd been spitting mad all day.

Barney hated car rides. She liked to spend the day on the back steps of their house in New York, watching a line of ants going back and forth. Sometimes she covered one with her paw. She always looked surprised when she raised her paw and the ant marched away.

Matthew followed his father down the driveway. Weeds had poked up in between the gravel. So had a few pink flowers. It was getting dark, so he couldn't see much, but the grass in the backyard was high, and the noise of the crickets loud.

"Wait a minute," his father said and stopped. "We can't go in through the side door." He smiled at Mrs. Jackson. "Front door, the first time."

He went up the walk and climbed the three steps

to the porch. "Looking good," he said. "Looking very good."

"Hurry." <u>Matthew</u> barely looked at the house. "I've got to go to the bathroom."

His father turned the key in the lock and pushed open the door. Behind him Mrs. Jackson hoisted Laurie up higher in her arms. She peered into the living room. "Good grief," she said. "It looks as if the moving men threw everything together in the middle of the floor."

Matthew rushed inside. He put Barney down on top of a box, then jumped over another one. "Where's the bathroom?"

His father pointed. "Top of the stairs."

Matthew ran up the stairs, his sneakers slapping against the bare wood. He closed the bathroom door, leaned against it, and looked at the walls. Pink wallpaper fish were swimming around in circles. Blue bubbles were coming out of their mouths.

Matthew tried a couple of spit bubbles in the mirror. "Not bad," he told himself.

Before he went downstairs again, he stopped to look at the furniture piled in the hall. He wondered how they'd ever get into the bedrooms tonight.

He pulled himself up on top of his mother's dresser and walked across on tiptoes. "I am zee fly man," he said. He tried to touch the ceiling. "I hang from zee walls and . . ."

He jumped across the night table and missed. He landed on the vacuum cleaner.

"Zee fly has crashed," he said. He rubbed his knee.

"What's going on up there?" his mother yelled. She was getting a little cranky, he thought.

He took the steps down two at a time, raced into the kitchen, and looked around.

Instead of fish blowing bubbles, there were tan coffeepots all over the wallpaper. Tons of them. The coffeepots were tipped over, pouring brown coffee into tan cups.

The countertops were tan and so were the cabinets.

"Yuck-o," he said.

THIS
SIDE
UP

"Double yuck-o," said his mother.

Right now, the coffeepots and the cabinets seemed to be flickering. His mother had put two pink candles on one of the counters. "Special," she said, "for our first meal here."

Everyone was sitting in a circle on the floor. His father was handing out slices of pizza.

Matthew sank down and reached for a piece. He took a huge bite. "I love this," he said.

"Close your mouth, Matthew," Cindy said. "You look like a cement mixer."

Matthew closed his mouth. He waited for her to look at him again. Then he opened his mouth wide and shut it.

"Gross," Cindy said. "The grossest thing I ever saw."

"Matthew," said his mother.

His father stretched. "First day of my new job is Monday. I'm glad it's Friday. I can spend the weekend painting."

Mrs. Jackson leaned back against the counter. Laurie was asleep in her lap, her thumb in her mouth. "We have to get things in shape. Cindy's twelfth birthday is Sunday. We'll have a cake, and sing, and maybe this place will feel like home. Look, I found the birthday plate."

Matthew looked at the old birthday plate. It was poking out of a box. If you wound up a little thing underneath the plate, it played "Happy Birthday." The plate would spin around slowly with the birthday cake on top.

At his last party they had played it a thousand times. His old friend Beast had been there, and Emily, and the rest of the kids from his class in the Polk Street School.

Good old Beast. Last week they had fixed up Beast's garage. They'd put a rug in the middle and an old chair. Beast had wanted him to hide there so he could stay in New York forever.

Matthew shook his head. How could anyone live in a garage by himself?

He stared at the birthday cake plate. He wondered if he'd ever see Beast or talk to him again.

10

"You'll see," his mother was saying. "It'll seem like home in no time."

"I'm going to hang the pictures right away," his father said. "That's the most important thing. It'll make it look like home."

Matthew glanced around the kitchen. Everything was strange in the candlelight. He thought about his old house. If only they were back there.

Then he thought about his plan. He had spent all day figuring it out. He wondered if he could make it work.

2

Next to the kitchen was the dining room. Matthew walked through it, jumping up to tap the bulb that hung on a cord from the ceiling.

He snapped his fingers. "Barney?"

She wasn't under the table that was shoved against the wall.

He went into the living room and lay down on the floor. He knew she was hiding underneath something.

Barney was a tough cat. When she was angry, she let you know it.

Matthew crawled around on the floor looking. After a minute he spotted her. She had backed herself behind the couch and was curled up in a lump against the wall.

He kneeled down to get as close as he could, wedging his head against the bottom of the couch. Then he reached underneath. He stretched his arm as far as he could.

"Matthew," his mother called from upstairs.

"Zee fly's arm is coming out of zee socket," Matthew said. He just about touched one of Barney's gray paws.

"Matthew," his mother yelled. "Right now."

Barney turned her head to look at him with yellow-green eyes. Then, slowly, she inched her way out.

"Gotcha," he said and picked her up. He could feel her heart thumping fast against his chest. Barney hated new places.

Matthew could hear his father hammering in the kitchen. He stopped at the bottom of the stairs to take a look.

Mr. Jackson was standing in front of the stove.

13

He reached over to hang a photograph over one of the wallpaper coffeepots.

The picture showed Laurie in her highchair. She was biting the bottom of a strawberry cone. Ice cream was running down her arm.

His father had moved the camera a little when he had taken the picture. The top of her head was missing.

Mr. Jackson turned his head to one side. "Great picture. Almost great anyway. That's what makes it home. Your own stuff all over the place."

Matthew stood there. He rubbed Barney's neck. He didn't think pictures would make this home. He couldn't think of anything that would.

His mother called again. "I don't have one drop of patience left."

"I think you'd better go upstairs," his father said.

Matthew climbed the stairs and started down the hall, jumping over a rolled-up rug. It was the only thing left on the floor. After supper his father had shoved everything else into the three bedrooms.

"Which one is mine?" Matthew asked. He hoped it would be the room at the end of the hall, the largest one.

"Up here." His mother's voice floated down from the attic. "I have a surprise."

Matthew stuck his head around the door that led up another flight. "Isn't that the attic?" he asked.

His mother came to the top of the stairs. "It isn't an attic really. There's a great bedroom up here. Come and look."

Matthew went up the stairs. He cleared his throat. "The ceiling comes to a point."

Mrs. Jackson nodded. "It's because of the roof. Isn't this a great place? Your father had a bedroom like this when he was your age . . . up at the top of the house. He knew you'd love it the minute he saw it."

Matthew didn't say anything. Barney jumped out of his arms and crawled under the bed.

"We'll fix the whole place up," Mrs. Jackson said. "We'll paint. You'll have friends stay over . . ."

"Maybe Cindy would rather have it," Matthew said, thinking that Cindy wouldn't stay up here for two minutes. It was probably the scariest room he had ever seen, away from the rest of the house. It was a big haunted attic.

"Your father saved this room for you," Mrs. Jackson said, looking around. "I can't find one blanket. Good thing it's a warm night." She flapped a sheet over the bed. It landed without a wrinkle.

Matthew looked around at the walls. Whoever lived here before must have loved tan paint. Even his bed with MATT scratched on it, and the toy chest filled with old games looked terrible in this room.

"Pajamas," his mother said. She hit her forehead with the back of her hand. "Where did the pajamas get to?"

"Don't worry," Matthew said. "I can sleep in my clothes."

Mrs. Jackson ran her hand through her hair. "I thought I had everything in that blue trunk."

"Maybe I should sleep in the hall tonight," Matthew said.

"Why?"

He stared up at the pointy ceiling. His mother didn't believe in ghosts or scary stuff.

"We're right downstairs," his mother said. "You and Barney will be fine." She kissed the top of his head and went down the stairs.

Matthew went over to the toy chest. It was just sitting there in the middle of the room. He shoved it against a wall.

He reached in his pocket for the wallet Beast had given him. Inside was the dollar from Cindy for his birthday, and Beast's fourteen cents.

He put the wallet and the police whistle Emily Arrow's father had given him on top of the chest. Lucky Emily. Her father was a policeman. The Arrows probably had police whistles all over the house.

Matthew went over and rolled onto the bed. A moment later he heard Barney scrambling out from underneath. She jumped up beside him and began to dig her claws into the pillow. In and out. In and out. She loved to do that.

Matthew wiggled his feet on the sheet, still in his sneakers. He watched the cat inch her way down to the end of the bed. She liked to pretend she was hunting. She dived for his laces.

Matthew leaned forward to give her tail a quick little tug.

She spun around, looking ferocious. Then she sat down and began to wash her paw.

Matthew sat back. That Barney was some cat. Her real name was Bonnie, but she was too tough for that.

He took a breath. It was time to think about his plan. The New Matthew plan. He was going to start all over in this place. He was going to be a new Matthew, a different Matthew.

Everyone here would think he was tough. He was *going* to be tough. No one would think he was afraid of anything. No one would know he used to wet his pants a long time ago, the way everyone in his old class had.

And smart. He was going to be smart. When he started school in the fall, he wouldn't answer any questions. No one would know he could hardly read. Everyone would think he was the smartest kid in the whole school.

He saw that the closet door was open a little. A black line ran down the side. It almost seemed as if the door were opening wider. He wouldn't look at it. He'd keep the light on all night.

"Matt?" His father called from the bottom of the stairs. "Great bedroom, right? Getting late. Better get those lights out."

Matthew got up off the bed. He ran across the room and slammed the closet door shut.

"Matt?" his father called.

"Great room." He took a breath. The new Matthew would never leave a light on. He punched the switch and dived for the bed.

He couldn't see anything, not one thing. Everything was black as a cave.

Barney moved closer to him. He reached out and rubbed her head. He still couldn't make her purr.

He was getting used to the dark now. He could see his toy chest, and the closet door, and a square patch of light from the window.

He knelt up in bed and looked out at the house next door. Somebody was jumping up and down in the bedroom directly across from his. Maybe it was a kid his own age. Maybe it was a kid who'd be in his class next fall. A great kid. Maybe he wouldn't even need the New Matthew plan.

Whoever it was came to the window.

"Hey," Matthew whispered.

The shade snapped down.

Some kid!

"Aiii," Matthew said in his scariest voice. He drew the sound out long and whispery. "Aiii."

The person bent over behind the shade. He pulled up the edge and peered out.

Matthew ducked down low. "Yaaaiiii," he moaned loudly.

21

Downstairs, Laurie started to cry.

"Matthew," his father shouted. "Stop that."

Matthew slid down in the bed. He pulled the sheet up over his head and Barney's.

3

It was morning. Matthew yawned and reached for Barney. She was gone, though. She must have gone downstairs for breakfast.

He went down the stairs to the bathroom. One good thing, he thought, he didn't have to get dressed. Maybe he'd sleep in his clothes from now on.

He turned on the cold-water faucet in the bathroom sink and bent down to take a sip. The water was hot. Nothing in this house worked right.

He leaned his nose against the mirror to watch his breath making steam. "Tough," he said under his breath. "Tough enough to tear telephone books."

He had seen a wrestler on television do that. The wrestler had picked up a telephone book. He had ripped it in half as if it were homework paper.

Matthew wondered where their telephone books were. He was going to work on that. Tear ten pages, then twenty. Soon he'd be able to rip the whole thing in half.

"Yes," he whispered into the mirror. "Zee man who rips buildings, who tears . . ."

Somebody banged on the bathroom door. Cindy. "I just got in here," he said.

He turned on the other faucet and let the water run. He splashed a little water on his face, then opened his mouth to check his teeth. They were big and curled on the ends. They were a little yellow too. Maybe he should start to use toothpaste.

He reached for his old blue toothbrush. It wasn't there, of course. There were a bunch of new ones.

Cindy was banging on the door again. He turned

24

the knob. Nothing happened. He tried again. "Hey, Cindy? Get Mom. The door is locked."

She pulled on the knob. "Did you twist that little thing?"

He had forgotten all about it. "Of course I did."

He waited a minute, then turned the lock. He tried out a New Matthew face, tough and hard, and opened the door.

Cindy was wearing one false eyelash. It looked like a caterpillar. "What's the matter with your face?" she asked. "It's all twisted or something."

"Just washed it," he said. "It's drying off." He raced down to the kitchen thinking he'd better practice his tough face in the mirror a little more.

His mother was standing at the sink, looking out the window. A million things were piled on the counters: plates, pots, knives, and nails, and even a living-room lamp.

Matthew took an apple off the windowsill. It had a bite out of one side . . . a little bite . . . a bite like Laurie's. He took a chunk from the other side. "Did you see Barney this morning?"

His mother shook her head, thinking. "I can't remember."

"I'll go out and look."

"Hold your horses. You have to eat breakfast."

"French toast?"

His mother smiled. "Don't be silly. I don't even have time to breathe. Take some orange juice out of the refrigerator . . ." She dabbed at a speck on the window. "I hope there's some in the refrigerator—and a piece of bread and butter."

Matthew pulled a slice of bread out of the bag. "It's the soft kind. Good. You can wad it right up into a baseball."

"Try wadding it up in your mouth," his mother said.

He washed the bread down with some juice and opened the back door. He had to remember to walk tough. He stuck his head up in the air, trying to make his neck look longer, and threw his shoulders back.

He went down the driveway, then stopped to look back at the house. It was even taller and skinnier than it had seemed last night. White paint was peeling all over the place. It had a great front porch, though. He had always wanted a front porch. He could sit out there even if it was raining.

He felt a lump in his chest. So what about a front porch? Without his friend Beast or Timothy, what good was it? He'd probably be sitting there all by himself like a big dummy.

"Barney," he called. He looked up and down the street. Houses on both sides, lots of bushes. She could be anywhere.

He tried to whistle. His whistles weren't very loud. That was another thing he'd have to practice. He'd never heard of a tough kid who couldn't whistle.

On the other side of his house was a grassy patch with bushes. It ran between his house and the house next door. He started back along it, still calling Barney.

The bushes were fat and green. He bent down and crawled into them. They were the sticky kind.

He pressed his hand against a branch. His fingers came away full of sap.

Everything was still wet, still cool. The bushes were so thick it was hard to see if Barney was around anywhere.

"Here kitty, kitty," he called. He crawled toward the backyard, watching out for spider webs.

In New York the spiders were okay. These might be full of poison. It was a great spy place, though. Beast would have loved it.

He and Beast had made up a terrific spy game. Sometimes they had crawled all the way down the block through the yards making believe they were after Lugo the Giant. There really wasn't any Lugo. They had just made him up to be the toughest guy in the world.

Matthew sat back on his sneakers and peered out. He could see part of his own yard, and next to it, separated by a skinny white fence, the next yard.

A kid was in the yard next door. It was probably the kid from last night. He was mounding dirt up

in a little pile, making noises, clicking his tongue against the roof of his mouth.

"C-lop, c-lip. Hole in one," he said.

Matthew tried a clopping noise too. It didn't come out exactly right.

The boy looked up.

Matthew ducked.

The boy picked up a hose and sloshed water into a hole. Matthew wondered why he would do that. The water would just sink into the earth.

He leaned forward to get a better look. The boy had almost no hair. What he did have was stuck up spiky, red, all over his head. He was smiling to himself. He had a real pumpkin face, with fat cheeks and teeth even bigger than Matthew's. Still holding the hose, he walked around his backyard.

He was closer now, close enough for Matthew to get a good look. He was the ugliest thing Matthew had ever seen, even uglier than Lugo.

The boy hopped the fence, pulling the hose behind him. He began to walk along the grassy area between the two houses.

Matthew pressed himself deeper into the bushes. He leaned against the house as hard as he could. The cement on the bottom dug into his back. He tried not to breathe.

The boy raised the hose. A stinging spray of water hit the bushes, then Matthew's head. "Yeow." Before he could move, his jeans and T-shirt were soaked.

The boy was laughing. He stood there slapping his knee, aiming the hose at Matthew.

"Cut that out," Matthew yelled. He crawled back toward the front of the house as fast as he could.

The hose followed him.

"Aii," the kid shouted. "Aiiiiiiii."

Matthew raced across the lawn. He pushed open the door.

Cindy was standing there. She blinked two caterpillar eyelashes. "Say one word," he told her, "and you're dead."

4

Matthew made a pass through the living room and into the dining room to check on Barney.

She wasn't in either room.

His father must have stayed up late last night, though. A horrible picture of Matthew was hanging on the wall. He was about a year old. He didn't have a hair on his head. He looked like a bald egg.

There was a picture of Cindy, too, when she was about four. She looked as if she had just eaten a lemon.

Matthew went into the kitchen, slicking down his wet hair. Laurie was sitting on the floor, pouring cereal onto the birthday plate. "Maffoo," she said, and shook the box.

He looked around to make sure no one was watching, then leaned over and kissed her. She was the greatest kid in the world. When she was a baby she had said his name first. At least it sounded like his name. Even Cindy said so.

His mother took the box out of Laurie's hands. "Give her some spoons, will you, Matt?" She reached out and touched the top of his head. "How did you get so wet?"

"Trying out the hose," he said, fingers crossed. He slid the birthday plate into an empty closet, and lined up four spoons on the floor. "I can't find Barney."

His mother frowned. "Wait until lunchtime. She never misses a meal."

"What's for lunch anyway?"

"Egg salad."

"With mayonnaise?"

"Of course. That's how you make egg salad."

"That's how I hate egg salad."

His mother leaned against the counter and rubbed her eyes. "It's not time for lunch yet anyway."

"How about a snack?"

"Why don't you go outside and play? There's a girl—what's her name?—I was talking with her mother before."

"I don't play with girls."

"You used to play with Emily Arrow."

"That was different." He broke off. "How come your eyes are all red?" Then he saw that his mother's eyes were filled with tears.

"It's hard to get used to a new house," she said slowly. "I miss the oak tree in back and the window in the dining room. I miss my friends."

Matthew stared at her. His mother never cried. Never. Well, maybe that one time in the park at home when she thought Laurie was lost. It was hard to think of his mother missing her friends.

He reached out to touch her arm. "Let's not get used to it. Let's pack right up, and when Dad comes home we can start to drive."

He pictured himself driving up his old block tomorrow morning. He'd get out of the car at Beast's house. Beast would be sitting on his front step with nothing to do and Matthew would say, "Want to take a dive in Emily's pool?" Something like that. As if he hadn't been away. Beast's eyes would almost fall out of his head, he'd be so surprised. They'd be jumping up and down, yelling. It would be the best thing that ever happened in his whole life.

"Let's go home," he told his mother. "Please let's go home."

His mother put her arms around him. "Matthew, I love you," she said.

They stood there for a moment, then Matthew looked out the screen door. He hoped that kid next door hadn't seen them.

His mother reached for a box of sugar wafers. She stuck one in Matthew's mouth. "We'll be fine right here. Really, Matt. You, and me, and Cindy, and Laurie. Everyone. Daddy has a wonderful new job. He's so happy about it . . ." She broke off. "How about doing a little work around here?"

"Like what?"

"Like taking these boxes down to the basement."

Cindy came into the kitchen. "He's afraid of the dark."

"I am not." He thought about making a tough face, but changed his mind. "I can't find Barney."

"She ate her food this morning," Cindy said. "Her bowl is empty."

Matthew nodded, relieved. "I looked outside. I didn't see her. If she goes too far, she'll get lost. She won't be able to find her way back."

Just then the phone rang. His mother reached for it. "Hi, Mom." She raised her eyebrows at Matthew. "Yes, we're all fine." She pointed with her foot to a bunch of shoe boxes. They were overflowing with his father's pictures. "Put them on the floor down there," she whispered.

Matthew opened the basement door and looked down the stairs. Even with the light on, it was al-

most dark. He stood on the top step and listened to his mother talking to his grandmother.

His grandmother had lived two doors away at their old house. She was always poking her head out the door, giving them cookies. He wondered when he'd ever see her again.

Matthew tried to see past the bottom step into the basement. He curled his lips and squinted his eyes. He tried to look as tough as he could, just in case someone was down there. "I have zee black belt in karate," he said.

"What?" Cindy asked.

"Nothing." He took a breath. The basement smelled awful. It looked awful too. Gray walls, gray floor. It was a terrible place. Maybe someone was buried down there.

Cindy stood in back of him. "Nothing's down there."

"I know that," he said. "What do you think, I'm crazy?"

"Use your head," Cindy said, blinking a little. "You just have to get used to this house."

"I think your own eyelashes looked better," he said.

She made a face. "I'm trying to look . . . I don't know. Better. Before anyone gets to know me."

"Want to earn some money?" he asked.

"How much?"

"Fourteen cents."

"You're a loon, Matthew."

"A dollar, I mean a dollar. I've still got the one you gave me for my birthday. Just take these boxes downstairs. I've got some stuff to do."

"Well . . ."

"The money's upstairs," he said. "On the toy chest."

He waited for her to nod, then headed down the hall toward the front door. He stuck out his chest, and shoved the door open. He put his head up high in the air, and walked across the porch.

He didn't see the top step. He slid down all three steps and landed on the walk.

The boy next door was watching. He had seen the whole thing.

"Did it on purpose." Matthew scrambled to his feet. "I'm so tough it doesn't bother me. Makes me tougher. Do it all the time."

The boy was swinging a stick around. He pointed it at Matthew. "Don't try anything."

"Poke someone's eye out like that," Matthew said.

"Does everyone in your house scream all the time?" the boy asked.

"Scream?" Matthew repeated. It was that stuff last night, he thought. He wished he hadn't made all those dumb *aiii* sounds. "Nobody screamed. It must have been someone else, some other house."

He tried to think of something else to talk about. "Where are the other kids around here?"

"Ballpark," the boy said, "or maybe the pool. I can't go swimming because my suit is ripped. Got to get a new one."

Matthew nodded. His bathing suit was packed

away somewhere. By the time they found it, it would be Christmas.

"Do you have a sister?" Matthew asked him.

The boy made the clopping sound. "You play with girls?"

Matthew tried a clopping sound too. "Of course not."

"I guess you don't know how to play golf," the boy said.

"Everybody knows how to play that," Matthew said. He tried to remember what golf was all about. He leaned over and looked under a bush next to the step. "I'm looking for my cat. She's gray with a little white."

"Probably in the park," the boy said. "We could go look for her." He stood up. "Except for the Wall."

"What wall?"

"It's a kid. A big, huge kid who gives everybody a bloody nose." The boy stared at the telephone pole in front of his house. "I had to have three stitches by him."

41

Matthew stared at the telephone pole too. He had gotten a stitch from a piece of glass. He had cried like a big baby. He knew he'd cry again. "How . . ."

The boy jumped off the steps. "I was trying to fight him with a stick." He shook his head. "You couldn't even beat that kid with . . ." He screwed up his eyes and tried to think. "With a bazooka gun. Anyway, I tried to run and . . ."

Matthew leaned forward.

The boy waved his hand. "Never mind. You'll see." He came across the lawn. "Why don't we go over to the park? See if we can find your cat now? I could be a lookout. Whistle if I saw the Wall coming."

Matthew stood up. He had to do it. Barney was probably lost, and scared.

"Just let me check the yard," he said.

They walked around the side of the house into the back.

"Needs mowing," the boy said.

Matthew nodded. It was easy to see that Barney

wasn't there. The bushes were low enough against the fence to see through. In the middle of the yard was a tree. Not bad for climbing, Matthew thought. Barney would love it for sharpening her claws. He'd have to tell his mother. Maybe it was even an oak tree.

"What's your name anyway?" the boy asked.

"Matthew J. Jackson," he said.

The boy spit on his hand. "Shake," he said. "I'm J.P. J.P. Peterson. Keep your fingers crossed we don't run into the Wall." He punched Matthew in the arm. "I'll be in your class at River Road."

Matthew swallowed. He hoped the Wall wouldn't get him first.

5

Matthew inched his way down Marita Street. He had a little smile on his face, and his arms were folded. He hoped he looked like Lugo the Giant.

Next to him J.P. was wearing a red kerchief over his nose. "Allergies," he said. "Can't go near a cat. Can't have one in the house. Sneeze my head off if I do."

Matthew wanted to look back over his shoulder. He wanted to see if the Wall was around. He was afraid to do it, though. His back felt like a bull's-eye. Any minute the Wall might come racing up and poke him with a stick.

He heard a crashing noise behind him. "Karate," he yelled, and spun around.

It was a woman with gray hair. She was putting out her garbage.

"Just practicing," Matthew said.

The woman smiled and put up her hands. "Any time you want boxing lessons let me know."

Matthew nodded.

"Wait behind the itchy-ball tree," J.P. told him. "I'll turn the corner and see if he's down the street."

"You think I'm afraid?" Matthew asked. "I was the toughest kid in my whole class. Even the garbage men were afraid of me."

J.P. didn't answer. He raced for the corner.

Matthew waited. He threw his head back, looking up into the tree. He made believe he was counting itchy balls, just in case the gray-haired woman was watching.

"Come on," yelled J.P.

Matthew turned the corner and ran to catch up

with J.P. If it weren't for Barney, he'd forget about this whole thing.

"So far, so good." J.P. waved his arm. "This way."

Matthew followed him through the park gates. They headed for the swings.

J.P. swung himself over a small fence and grabbed a swing. He rattled the chain as hard as he could. "This is it. Best park in the world."

Matthew walked around the fence and sat on the edge of the next swing. He looked around. The best park in the world wasn't so great.

There were no trees, no bushes, no place for a cat to hide. A hot breeze swirled across the cement. It sent an empty soda can rattling away from them.

He could see the whole park. Across the way were a couple of slides and a sandbox. Next was a picnic area with benches. Beyond that was the ballfield. A bunch of boys were tossing a ball back and forth, but it was too far to see what they looked like.

"My cat isn't here," he told J.P. Poor Barney.

He wondered where she was. She was probably trying to look tough wherever she was. By now she must be hungry, though. Barney liked to eat a lot.

Matthew pushed back on the swing as hard as he could. He sailed forward, eyes closed. He didn't want J.P. to see he was almost crying. "The swings where I live . . ." he began.

"You live here," J.P. said.

". . . have rubber seats. Not tin that burns half your legs off."

J.P. gave a swing a huge push. With no one on it, the swing zigzagged back and forth wildly.

"Watch out," Matthew yelled.

J.P. waited for the swing to slow down. Then he jumped on the seat. "Sorry about your cat," he said. "I thought she might be here."

Matthew nodded. He slowed his swing with his foot.

"Want to race?" J.P. asked.

Matthew shook his head. J.P. knew all about these swings. He'd probably win. "No."

"How many kids in your family?" J.P. asked.

47

"Three. Me, Laurie, and . . ."

"And that girl." J.P. slid down on the swing seat and pumped hard. "The one with a face full of freckles. She was reading a book on the steps this morning. Early."

Matthew nodded. "That's Cindy."

"Don't read much myself," said J.P.

"Me neither," said Matthew. He let his head fall back. Everything was upside down. He wouldn't read. He'd make believe he couldn't talk. The teacher would never find out . . .

Good idea, except it would never work.

"Oh, oh," J.P. said.

Matthew dragged his sneakers along the cement to stop the swing. "What's the matter?"

"Listen. He's coming," J.P. said.

Matthew swallowed. "How do you know?"

"I just heard him whistle." J.P. opened his mouth. He curled his tongue behind his bottom teeth. He let out a piercing whistle. It was much louder than Matthew could do. "Like that."

"Ssh. Want him to hear you?"

J.P. pointed toward the park gates. "Take a look. He'll be here any minute."

Matthew jumped off the swing. "I think it's time to go home now. Is there another way out?"

"Yeah. On the other side." J.P. yanked at his shoulder. "There he is."

Matthew turned. He drew in his breath. Coming through the open gates were two kids. Matthew could see which one the Wall was. He was wearing a red sweatshirt and jeans. He looked big and square like Matthew's uncle's pickup truck.

"Ya, ya. Ya, ya," J.P. shouted.

The Wall turned to look at them.

"You can't get us," J.P. yelled. He was dancing up and down.

For a moment Matthew couldn't move. The Wall looked tougher than anyone he had ever seen. A whole lot tougher than the New Matthew.

The Wall took a step toward them.

J.P. took off. He jumped over the low fence, circled the slides, and sped across the park.

Matthew took a quick breath. Then he ran too.

He followed J.P. across the ballfield and out the gates on the other side of the park.

Behind him, the Wall was yelling, "If I get my hands on you, Jennifer Peterson, you'll be sorry."

6

Matthew couldn't stop yawning. His second night in the new house had been worse than the first.

It was terrible sleeping without Barney. It was terrible wondering where she was.

He went outside and walked slowly around the house. "Come on, Barn," he called. He looked under all the bushes on the side of the house. Then he wandered around the backyard.

He looked across at J.P.'s house. That J.P. was crazy. Jennifer Peterson.

What was the matter with her anyway, trying to make him think she was a boy?

He was never going to bother with her again.

His father stuck his head out of the attic window. "If you want your room done first, you'd better get that paint up here."

Matthew looked up. He shielded his eyes with his hands. "On my way."

He raced into the garage, grabbed the can of blue paint, and went in the back way.

Cindy was in the living room. She was leaning on her elbows, reading. "I read about a cat one time," she said. "A cat who was lost and tried to get home."

Matthew ran his tongue over his lips. "Did she get home?"

Cindy nodded. "Her family was there waiting for her."

Matthew swallowed. He thought about Barney trying to get home to New York. It was the worst thing he could think of. Cars whizzing along the highway. She was so small. Suppose she was lost, or hurt?

Matthew went up the fourteen steps to his bedroom with the paint. Blue paint.

He had picked it out himself at the hardware store last night. It wasn't that baby blue stuff. It was good and dark and strong-looking.

His father was on top of a ladder. He was painting the ceiling white. His mother was sitting on the floor, scrubbing the molding. She leaned over to look at the paint. "Wow. It hurts my eyes."

"You don't like it?"

"Of course I do," she said. "Nothing wrong with a nice bright color."

"That's what I always say," said Mr. Jackson.

"Cindy said she read about a cat," Matthew said. "It got lost somehow. It tried to find its way home."

His mother ran her hand over the wall. "What a mess—" She broke off. "I remember that book. *Incredible Journey.* It was wonderful. Maybe it was even true."

"You think a cat could find its way home?"

"I think a cat might try." She sat back on her heels. "You're thinking of Barney."

Matthew nodded.

"Don't give up on her yet. I put food out on the back steps this morning. It's gone now."

"It could be any cat who's eating it."

"I guess it could," his mother said.

"I bet it's old Barney," said his father.

"Maybe." Matthew took a breath. He didn't want to think about Barney lost and crying anymore. "Let's paint."

"Wait awhile," his mother said. "First we have to finish washing the walls. I'll start one wall. You can start another."

"I hate that part," Matthew said. "Who's going to know if the walls are clean underneath?"

"Everybody will know. New paint won't stick to dirty walls."

"Oh." Matthew dipped a sponge into a pail of soapy water. He began to run it along the wall. Across the way, J.P. had come outside. She was tearing up the grass with her golf club again. She stopped and looked up at his window.

Matthew ducked away and looked at the wall. He could see there was too much water on the sponge. Two drops of water raced each other down the wall, leaving tan streaks. "Suppose there's a big kid around here?" he asked.

"Lots of big kids all over," his father said.

"I mean really big and mean."

His mother looked over. "Make friends. Do that right away. Go up to the kid, shake hands, and say 'I'm Matt. I'm looking for a friend.' "

Matthew dabbed at his sneaker tops with the sponge. They were soaking wet. He could never go up to a kid like that and shake hands. The Wall would probably squeeze his hand off.

"Whatcha doin'?" a voice asked a minute later.

J.P. She was standing in the doorway, hands on her hips. "Got an extra sponge?" she asked. "This place is one mess. Sooner everybody gets together, sooner it gets done."

"How did you get in here?" Matthew asked.

"Poked my nose in the back door. Cindy said I could come up."

Mrs. Jackson tossed her a sponge. "Great to see you. We've got a wall for you to wash."

J.P. dipped the sponge into the bucket of water. She started to scrub the wall. Drops of water flew all over the place. She kept looking at Matthew out of the corner of her eye.

Matthew made believe he didn't notice.

"It's great that you guys are here," she said. "Not one kid my age on this whole block until Matthew moved in."

Matthew snorted a little. He wrung out his sponge.

"I was a little afraid," J.P. said. "Figured Matthew might be the kind of kid who wouldn't play with girls."

Mrs. Jackson smiled. "Matthew was good friends with Emily Arrow in our old neighborhood."

Matthew leaned closer to the wall. He made believe he was checking out the spots.

"Hey, that's great," J.P. said. She grinned at Matthew.

He picked at a little dot of dirt on the wall. Actually J.P. didn't look so bad when she smiled. The whole thing was sort of funny, thinking she was a boy. He couldn't help smiling a little.

"Want to race?" she asked. "See who can finish their wall first?"

Matthew started to work as fast as he could.

"Did you tell everyone about that kid?" J.P. asked.

"You mean the Wall?" Matthew said.

Mrs. Jackson began to laugh. "The Wall?"

"Not his real name, of course," J.P. said. "That's what we call him."

"What's his real name?"

"Warren. Warren Peterson."

Matthew stared at her. "What do you mean— Peterson?"

J.P. squeezed the sponge over her head. "Hot as baked beans in here."

"What do you mean . . ." Matthew began again.

"He's my brother," she said. "But don't think that will help you. He's the worst kid I ever knew in my life."

7

At supper that night Matthew looked at his hands. They were blue. He had spots of blue paint on his arms too. "Zee blue man," he whispered to himself.

"Matthew," J.P. screeched from the alley. A moment later she stuck her nose against the screen door. "Can I come in?"

"Sure," Mrs. Jackson said. She tried to put a piece of hamburger into Laurie's mouth. "If only this kid would eat something once in a while. She lives on air."

Laurie spit the meat out of her mouth. She smiled at Matthew.

"Give her some more of that cat food," J.P. said. "She loves it."

Everyone looked up. "Cat food?" Mrs. Jackson asked.

J.P. pointed over her shoulder with her thumb. "On the back step. She ate it while you were putting the garbage out."

"Good grief," Mrs. Jackson said.

Cindy pushed her hair back. "She had brown stuff all over her mouth while I was watching her this afternoon."

"Gross," said J.P.

"If Laurie's eating Barney's food . . ." Matthew began and stopped. That meant that Barney hadn't been around here at all today, or even yesterday. It was the end of Barney, he thought. She was really gone.

He didn't want to think about it. He couldn't eat one more mouthful. He pushed his chair back. "Let's go," he told J.P. He opened the screen door and looked back.

Cindy was saying something. She was asking

how long a cat could live without food. His mother was wiping her eyes as she lifted Laurie out of her high chair. His father was shaking his head. His eyes looked sad too.

Matthew followed J.P. into her yard. "We'll make a pile of holes," she said. "It will make the golf game better."

Matthew picked up a trowel. If he thought about putting golf holes in the lawn, he couldn't think about Barney.

A few minutes later his mother and father came outside with Laurie. "Going to look for a new stove," his father called. "The stores are open late."

Matthew nodded and started another hole. He looked up toward the Petersons' windows. J.P. had told him which one was the Wall's.

"Don't worry." J.P. rubbed her dirty hands on her jeans. "He's not up there. He's holed up in the garage. I don't know what he's been doing in there all day. He could be building a bomb for all I know."

She bent over and picked up a stone. "Watch." She tossed it against the garage.

A moment later the Wall came to the window. Matthew could see that his hair was as spiky as J.P.'s. He had fat cheeks like J.P.'s, and brown eyes.

He looked mean. Even meaner than Drake Evans in Matthew's old school.

The Wall pushed up the window. He stuck his head out. Matthew wondered why he didn't come sailing right out onto the Petersons' lawn.

"You trying to start something again?" the Wall yelled to J.P.

She jumped up and down. She began to make gorilla noises.

The garage window slammed down.

"He's coming after us," J.P. yelled.

Matthew looked at his back door. It would take him about two seconds to get inside and lock the screen.

The Wall could bash through it in nothing flat.

"Don't worry," J.P. said. "We can take him. You said you're tougher than the garbage man."

The garage door swung open. The Wall charged out.

"Run for your life," J.P. yelled. She took a flying leap over a rosebush.

Matthew raced for the back door. He opened the screen, went in, and locked it. Then he dashed for the stairs.

Someone was in back of him, coming fast.

He pulled open his bedroom door. He slammed it behind him, and leaned against it. His hair stuck to the back of the door.

He had forgotten about the paint. His T-shirt was sticking to it, too, wet and cold.

Someone banged on the door. The noise drummed in his ears. He could hardly breathe. If only he were back in New York, back in his old house.

"Matthew. Open the door."

"Cindy?"

"Who do you think? Godzilla? Are you all right?"

He took a breath and peeled himself off the door. He looked back at it. The new paint was a mess.

"It's okay," he yelled to Cindy. "Don't worry."

He listened to her going back down the stairs.

Then he stood in the middle of the room, arms out, away from his shirt. Somehow there was paint on the front of it too. He waited for his heart to stop pounding.

8

Matthew peeled off his T-shirt and threw it in the corner. He tiptoed to the window.

Across the way the screen door banged open. A woman came outside. She had spiky hair like J.P.'s. She cupped her hands around her mouth. "Jennifer. Warren."

She stood there, shaking her head. Then she went into the house again.

Matthew stayed at the window. He'd be here for the rest of his life, living next door to J.P. and Warren the Wall.

He closed his eyes. If only he could find Barney. If only he could talk to Beast.

If only he could call him. How could he do that though? Cindy would listen. If his mother and father were home they might listen too.

Everyone would think he was the world's worst baby if they heard what he wanted to tell Beast.

Matthew thought for a moment. He went over to his dresser and opened it with two fingers, trying not to get paint on the drawer.

He pulled out his oldest T-shirt. It was blue. No one would even notice he had paint all over him. He yanked it on and looked at the toy chest.

His fourteen cents was still there. So was the dollar. Cindy hadn't taken it for carrying the boxes downstairs for him yesterday.

Good old Cindy.

Outside someone was whistling. He looked out the window again. It was J.P. She jumped over a golf club and headed for her back steps.

The Wall was right behind her. He didn't go into the house, though. He went down the driveway. Then he glanced back over his shoulder. As he pushed up the garage doors it looked as if he were talking to himself.

The door slammed down behind him.

"Sneaky-looking kid," Matthew said to himself. He scooped the money off the toy chest. It probably wasn't enough.

He went down the stairs. Cindy was on her bed reading. "Your head is blue," she said.

"Lend me some money?" he asked.

Cindy looked worried. "You're not going to run away, are you?"

"No."

"A loan," she said. "Only a loan."

"Of course, what do you think?" He took a pile of change off her dresser.

"Good-bye, money," said Cindy.

He ducked his head. "I'll give it back."

He went downstairs and outside. It was getting dark. He could see lights in the Petersons' living room. He wondered if the Wall was really building a bomb in the garage. He went past their house quickly and turned the corner. He remembered passing a candy store on the way to the park with J.P.

In front of the store was a phone booth. He said his old number under his breath: 555-9442. Beast's was 555-0433.

He looked down at the dollar in his hand. Then he went into the candy store. "Can I have . . ."

"Frozen Milky Way bar?" a man with a mustache asked.

"Change."

The man slid four quarters across the counter.

"How about five?" Matthew asked.

"How about you learn to add?" said the man.

Matthew didn't stop to argue. As long as he had enough to call, he was all right.

Matthew went back to the phone booth and reached into his pocket. He put Cindy's money up on the shelf and his own.

Then he picked out a dime and dialed the operator. She'd have to do that area code stuff for him. He got ready to drop the money into the slots.

It was easier than he thought. A few minutes

later Beast's phone began to ring. Matthew even had a quarter and a dime left.

The phone rang three times.

Suppose Beast wasn't there?

Then a voice answered. "Hello." It was Beast's sister, Holly.

"Get Beast," he said.

"Matthew, is that you?" Holly screamed. "Richard, hurry up. It's Matthew calling all the way from Deposit, Ohio. Run."

Matthew held the phone away from his ear. Then Beast was on the phone. He sounded as if he were right there, right in the phone booth with him. "Hey, Beast," he said.

"Hey, Matthew," Beast said at the same time. "Did you get my letter?"

"Not yet," Matthew said.

"That's right. I just mailed it this morning. You'll get it Monday, I guess."

"Good," said Matthew. "I meant to write to you. I will. Really."

Then for a moment, he couldn't think of anything else to say.

"How's the weather out there?" Beast asked.

"Listen," Matthew said. "Barney's missing. Maybe she's trying to get home."

For a minute Beast didn't answer. Matthew could almost hear him thinking. "I'll go right over there now," Beast said. "I'll bring some water. Water with ice cubes. I remember she likes it that way. Don't worry. I'll keep watching. It may take her a while." He stopped. "Matthew? What's the matter?"

Matthew shook his head. His eyes were watering. "Nothing." He took a breath. "There's this kid. He's strong as an ox. He's after me."

"After you? Why?"

Matthew raised one shoulder in the air. "I don't know."

Beast cut in. "Isn't he a kid like the ones around here?"

"I don't think so."

"Listen," Beast said. "Stay in the house."

"Forever?" Matthew said.

"I guess not." Beast took a breath. "You've got to figure out a way to get him on your side. Look tough, Matthew. Tougher than he is."

Just then there was a click in the phone. "I've got to hang up." Another click. "Look for Barney," he yelled.

"Don't worry," Beast yelled back. "Good luck . . ."

Matthew put the phone down again. He could almost see Beast running over to his old house. Running with water and food.

Then he straightened his shoulders. It wasn't his old house anymore. It was someone else's.

He still felt terrible, but Beast would be his friend forever. It was a great thought. Even if Beast was in China, even if Beast was in California, they'd still be best friends. He was going to tell him that as soon as he could.

Beast probably knew it already.

It was nice to know that Beast would look out for Barney. If Barney ever made it.

9

It was Sunday morning, their third day.

"Please walk Laurie," Mrs. Jackson said. "Take her off my hands while I make Cindy's birthday cake. You'll be my best friend for life."

"I guess so." Matthew waited while she put Laurie into the stroller. She stuffed Patty Cake, her doll, in too.

"Here's some money for a treat," said Mrs. Jackson. "No candy, please."

Matthew started up the street pushing the stroller in front of him. He kept his head down and watched the cement whiz past underneath.

Laurie was singing, "La, la, la." She kept time by banging Patty Cake on the head.

She was making more noise than a jet plane.

His mother opened an upstairs window. "Matthew? Why don't you take her to the park? She might like that."

Laurie turned around in her stroller to look up at him. "Park, Maffoo, park."

Matthew waved at his mother. He kept going down the street.

Laurie was yelling, "Park," at the top of her lungs.

Matthew thought about going through the park gates. He thought about meeting up with the Wall. Get it over with, he told himself.

He tried to remember what he knew about fighting. He stopped the stroller and stood back. He put his arms out in front of him the way those black-belt guys on TV did. He chopped them around. "He ha," he said under his breath.

"He ha," said Laurie in front of him.

His mouth was so dry he could hardly swallow.

He stood up as straight as he could. He tried to look like the New Matthew. He tried to look as tough as Drake Evans from his old school.

He looked down at his hands on the stroller. The Wall would think he was some big baby, walking his sister around a ballfield.

So what? That's what Drake Evans would say. That's what the New Matthew would say too.

Matthew went through the park gates. The Wall wasn't there. Some other kids were playing ball, though. One of them even waved at him.

Matthew waved back. He walked Laurie around the path a couple of times, then he went out of the park and turned the corner.

In front of him, up ahead, was the Wall. Spiky hair up in the air. Huge. He was halfway up the block, coming out of the supermarket, walking away from Matthew. He was carrying a big bag of stuff. Heavy stuff. He was bent backward.

Matthew slowed up. He could wait. The Wall would never see him.

"Candy," said Laurie. She pointed at the supermarket. "Red."

Good. That would take enough time to let the Wall get far away.

"How about cookies?" he told Laurie. He wheeled the stroller up to the door and waited for it to swing open. Coward, a voice said inside him. Big coward.

He took his time looking at the stacks of cookies. Behind him two women were talking. "These kids," said one of them. "Now they're painting their hair. I can't believe it."

Matthew wondered who would do a thing like that. He tried to picture Cindy in pink hair. Then he remembered the blue paint. The women must be talking about him. He grabbed a box of animal crackers. "Come on," he told Laurie. "Let's get out of here."

He paid for them and watched Laurie smile. She smiled so hard her eyes were little crinkles in her cheeks. She opened her mouth wide and waited for Matthew to rip the paper open.

He found a lion cracker for her. Then he tucked the box next to her in the stroller.

Laurie chewed the cracker with her mouth open. She was still smiling at him.

Laurie thought he could do anything. How terrible it would be when she grew up a little. She'd find out he was a big coward.

Outside he could still see the Wall. He was almost at the end of the next block.

Matthew was sick of being a coward, sick of being afraid. He started to walk, moving faster. No more coward, he told himself.

He was almost running now. Patty Cake fell out of the stroller.

He bent down to pick up the doll. He raced down the street with Patty Cake in one hand, the stroller bouncing in front of him.

"Faster, Maffoo," Laurie was yelling. "Faster."

The Wall heard them and turned.

Matthew tried to put on his tough New Matthew face. It didn't seem to work, though. He moved the stroller out of the way. "You want to fight?" he asked. He could hardly get the words out.

The Wall looked surprised. His mouth opened in a fat round O.

"I'm ready," Matthew said.

"Ready?"

"To fight."

The Wall tried to get a better grip on his grocery bag. "J.P.," he said. "Did she start this?"

Matthew took a step back. He put Patty Cake in the stroller. "J.P.?"

The Wall started to laugh. "It was J.P., wasn't it? That kid's been trying to get back at me ever since those stitches."

"She said . . ." Matthew began.

"That kid is crazy. She came after me with a stick. I started to chase her. Next thing she fell over a rock." The Wall shook his head. "I've been trying to tell her all summer . . ."

He hoisted the bag a little. The bottom tore.

A bunch of red cans dropped onto the cement.

"Yeow," yelled the Wall. The cans rolled into the street.

The Wall bent over, trying to gather everything up.

Matthew stood there a moment, watching the Wall scrambling around in the street. Suddenly he felt better, a lot better. "Let me help," he said.

He bent down and picked up a can. "Tuna Tasties for Terrific Cats," it said.

Matthew grabbed a second can. "Liver Platter for Liver Lovers." Barney hated that kind. She'd never eat it. Not in a million years. "My cat hates . . ." he began.

He had a quick flash of J.P. in his mind. J.P., a red kerchief over her nose because she was allergic to cats. "I thought you couldn't have a cat in your house," he said.

The Wall grabbed another can. "We can't. J.P.'s allergic. The cat's in the garage."

"But . . ."

"Don't tell her," the Wall said. "Don't tell anyone. I found this cat. That's why I had to get all this food. I don't know what she likes."

Matthew looked at the Wall. He didn't look tough, not tough at all. He looked worried.

Matthew picked up the last can. He turned it in his hands. He couldn't believe it. His eyes were tearing again. He swallowed hard, trying to get the words out, even though he knew the answer. "What color is the cat?" he said at last.

10

It was Sunday, almost time for Cindy's birthday dinner.

Matthew licked the point of his pencil. He began to write.

Hapy Berthday, Cindy.

No. That didn't look right.

He crumpled up the paper and tossed it across the bedroom floor.

Barney opened one eye. She didn't bother to move. Sometimes she loved to chase paper, other times she was too lazy.

Matthew sat down next to her on the floor and

leaned against the bed. Wait till Beast heard the news. He was going to write a letter right after dinner.

Next to him, Barney began to purr. Matthew closed his eyes and thought back to yesterday.

"Gray," the Wall had said. "The cat is gray. She's tough, too, climbing all over the place."

Then the Wall had seen Matthew's face. He knew Matthew was crying. He must have known. Matthew didn't even make believe something was in his eye. He didn't care about being the New Matthew anymore. He was so glad Barney was safe. He was so glad that no matter what, he was going to get her back, and pet her, and give her water with ice cubes or whatever she wanted.

And that's just what had happened. They had piled the cans in Laurie's stroller and zoomed down the street toward the Wall's garage. The Wall had talked nonstop. "I'm so glad it's your cat," he kept saying. "I didn't know how I was going to keep her."

The Wall didn't even seem as tough as J.P.

They had raced up the driveway, and the Wall ducked down to slide the garage doors up.

And there she was, sitting on a soft white pillow.

"My bed pillow," the Wall said. "I had to sneak it out of the house."

"Here, killy, killy, killy," Laurie said.

Barney looked up at Matthew and began to purr.

"Laurie can't say 'kitty' right." Matthew tried to explain, but he couldn't get the words out. He picked up Barney and buried his face in the soft fur of her neck. . . .

Matthew's father called from downstairs. "Hurry, Matt. You're holding up the works."

Matthew jumped. He reached for another piece of paper.

> Hapy Berthday, Cindy.
> I O you a presint.
> I will get you something grate
> as soon as I get mor mony.
> > Your bruther,
> > Matthew J. Jackson

He looked around for an envelope, even though he knew he'd never find one. He folded the paper in half and stuck it in his pocket. Then he headed downstairs.

On the top step he looked back at his room. The blue paint looked bright. Shimmery. Matthew had never seen a blue room like that before. It was because the paint was boat paint. His father had told him.

It was turning out to be a great bedroom.

Matthew went down the stairs into the kitchen. Everyone was there. His mother was putting little yellow candles on the cake. His father was getting his camera ready to take pictures. Laurie was holding Patty Cake. Patty had smudges on her face from where the stroller had run over her, but his mother had fixed her up almost as good as new. She was still working on getting the blue paint out of his hair.

Cindy sat at the head of the table. She had a pile of presents in front of her. Matthew slid the note underneath.

Cindy was wearing the caterpillar eyelashes. She blinked them at him and smiled. "It's great to be twelve," she said. "I may even be able to get a grown-up library card."

Mrs. Peterson was sitting at the other end of the table. She was nodding at Cindy.

On the other side of the table was J.P. She was wearing a red kerchief on her nose. Next to her was the Wall. It was going to be hard to remember to call him Warren.

And Barney. Barney had followed him downstairs. Now she was curled up on the refrigerator, one eye closed, watching them with the other one.

That's exactly what she had done yesterday when Matthew and the Wall had brought her home.

The Wall was turning out to be a great kid. He hadn't even thought it strange when everyone in the house started to cry as soon as they saw Barney. "It's been a crying family," his mother had told him, "but I think we're all right now."

Matthew thought they were all right too. Besides, there'd be a letter from Beast tomorrow. And he was going to write too, tonight. His mother had said that maybe Beast's mother would let him come on a plane to visit them. He'd ask about it when he wrote. He knew Beast would drive his mother crazy until she said yes.

Mrs. Jackson brought the cake to the table.

"Hold everything," said their father. He stood up on a chair and began to snap pictures. "First birthday in the new house. We'll look back and remember it forever."

His mother smiled. She wound up the old birthday plate. It began to play "Happy Birthday" and turn slowly.

Matthew looked around the table. Then he opened his mouth and began to sing.

About the Author

Patricia Reilly Giff is the author of over thirty books for young readers, including the Kids at the Polk Street School books, the New Kids at the Polk Street School books, and the Polka Dot Private Eye books. A former teacher and reading consultant, she holds degrees from Marymount College and St. John's University, and a Professional Diploma in Reading from Hofstra University.

Mrs. Giff lives in Weston, Connecticut.

About the Illustrator

Blanche Sims has illustrated all Patricia Reilly Giff's Polk Street School books. She lives in Westport, Connecticut.